About the Author:

Dr. Daniela Owen is a psychologist in the SF Bay Area who brings to life healthy mind concepts and strategies for children everywhere. For more about the author please check out: drdanielaowen.com

For Lila Skye and Milo Grant

ISBN: 978-1-953177-45-2

Edition: September 2020

For all inquiries, please contact us at:
info@puppysmiles.org

To see more of our books, visit us at:
www.PuppyDogsAndIceCream.com

This book is given with love...

_____

_____

Sometimes we just want to think about ourselves.

We want,
what we want...

We want to do,
what we want to do...

And we don't want to
think about other people.

But, we live in a world
with lots of other people.

Many of us have
families at home...

Classmates and teachers

in our schools...

And friends in our neighborhoods, towns, and cities.

It's important
to be aware of and kind
to all of these other people.

When we pay attention
to other people, it helps us to be
more aware of our own actions.

And our actions are important
because they can affect others.

There are a few simple ways
to be mindful of our actions
and to be good, kind citizens
in our communities...

Whether it's in our homes,
in our neighborhoods,
or in our schools.

The first way to be kind

is to look around you and be aware

of other people wherever you go.

When you notice who's around you,
you can see whether
you need to change your actions
based on those other people.

A second way to be kind

is to ask people

if they need any help.

Even though you may prefer
to do something else,
after a short time
you will find joy
in helping others.

Contributing makes us feel
more valuable as people.

And the people we help

will really appreciate it.

A third way to be kind
is to show people you care
through random acts of kindness.

When we think about people
in our community
and do kind things for them
(even if they didn't ask us to)
we feel connected to them.

Try looking around you and seeing
if there are any kind things
that you can do...

Like putting toys away,
giving a thoughtful gift,
or taking care of a pet.

Sometimes it can take
extra time and effort to notice
what's happening around us
and to do something helpful.

But practicing this is worth it,
because caring for those
in our communities
turns us into kind people.

So remind yourself...

Right now, I am kind!

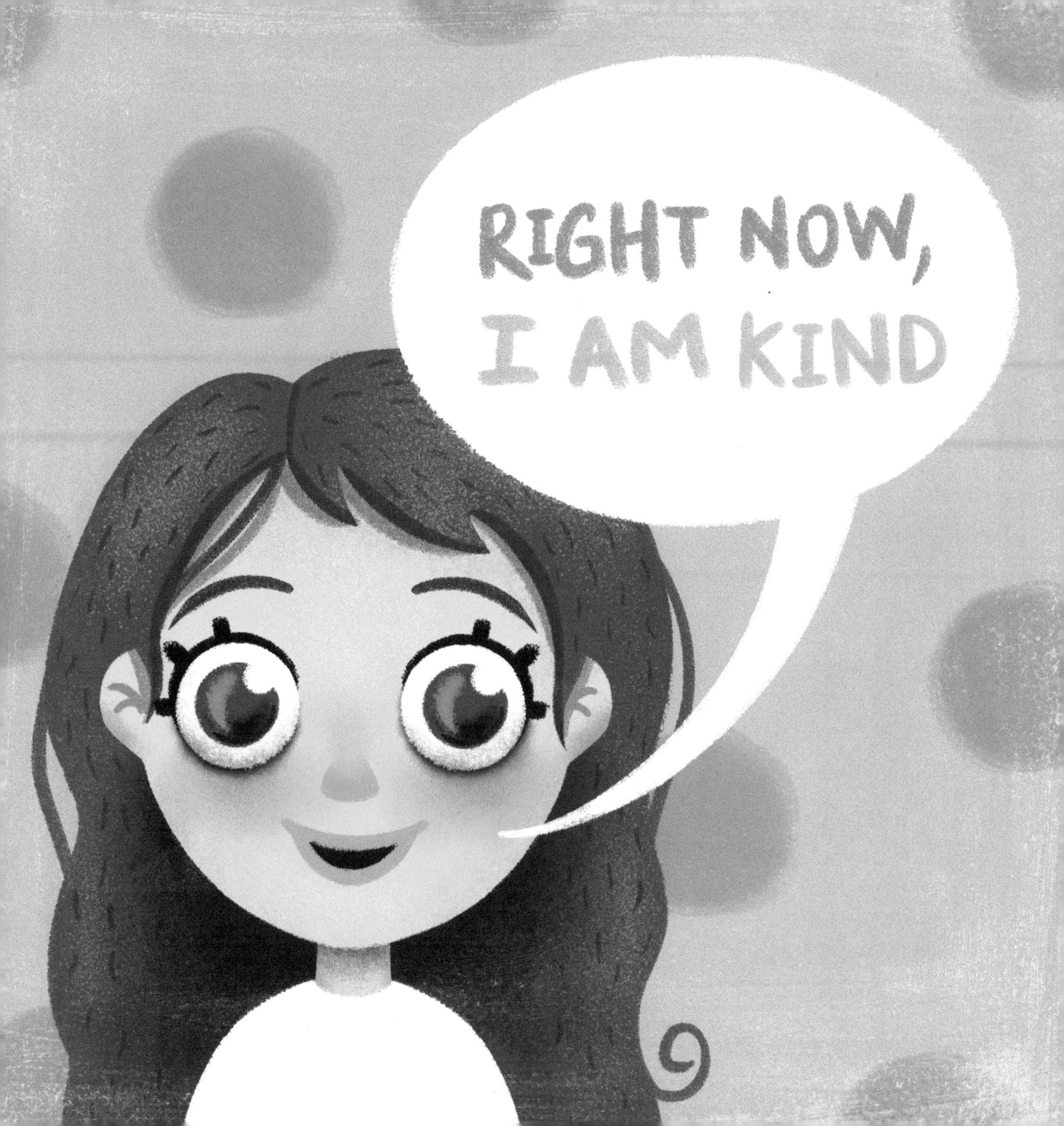
RIGHT NOW,
I AM KIND

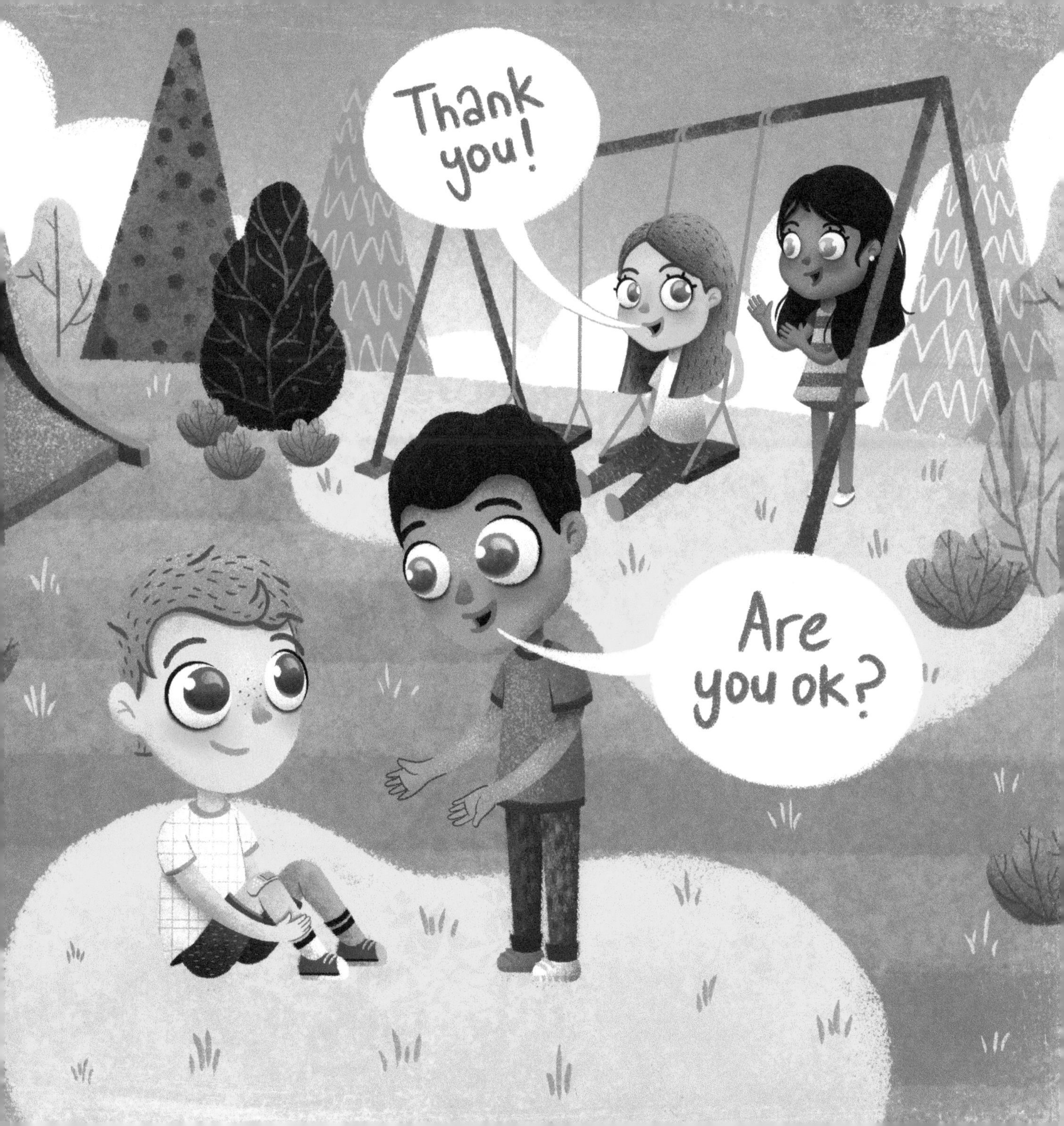
Thank you!
Are you ok?

CPSIA information can be obtained
at www.ICGtesting.com
Printed in the USA
BVHW020905040421
603833BV00005B/11